MOLLY AND THE SHIPWRECK

To Coillín, my beautiful light.
AW

Molly and the Shipwreck published by Graffeg in 2021.
Copyright © Graffeg Limited 2021.

ISBN 9781913733919

Text © Malachy Doyle, illustrations © Andrew Whitson,
design and production Graffeg Limited. This publication
and content is protected by copyright © 2021.

Malachy Doyle and Andrew Whitson are hereby identified
as the authors of this work in accordance with section 77 of
the Copyrights, Designs and Patents Act 1988.

A CIP Catalogue record for this book is available from the
British Library.

Assisted by Donegal County Council and Creative Ireland.

Mali a'r Llongddrylliad (Welsh edition) ISBN 9781914079566
Muireann agus an Longbhriseadh (Irish edition)
ISBN 9781912929221

Teaching Resources
www.graffeg.com/pages/teachers-resources

1 2 3 4 5 6 7 8 9

THIS BOOK BELONGS TO

_____

_____

_____

_____

MALACHY DOYLE ANDREW WHITSON
MOLLY AND THE SHIPWRECK

GRAFFEG

A few days after Molly's friend Nan and her family left to go and live on the mainland, a letter came home from Miss Ellie, Molly's teacher.

'Oh no!' said Molly's mother. 'It says the school might be closed down unless we can find some more children.'

'But it's an island, Mum!' cried Molly. 'There aren't any more!'

So Molly stopped the day-trippers on their way back to the boat.

'Did you like my island?' she asked them. 'Would you like to live here and go to my school?'

And they all said it was lovely – but they'd really rather go home, if Molly didn't mind.

A few weeks later, Molly was out fishing with her father when a very different kind of boat arrived.

'Look, Dad!' yelled Molly. 'Over there!'

It was a rickety old thing, and it looked like the people in it were in real trouble.

'Help!' a woman was shouting. 'Help! Help!'

Molly and her dad somehow managed to get them into his little red fishing boat and turned for home.

After Molly's mum cooked them up a hot meal, the oldest child, Amina, showed Molly some pictures of where they'd come from.

'*Mamá...*' said Amina. '*A mi papi...*' she added, sadly.

'Your dad?' said Molly. 'Where is he now? Did you have to leave him behind?'

'Shush, Molly,' said her mother. 'Give the girl some peace.'

'Would you like to stay here?' Molly asked Amina. 'Would you like to live on my island?'

'You're sweet to offer, love,' said Molly's mum. 'But I don't think they'd be allowed. I think they'll have to go to the camp on the mainland.'

Molly had other ideas, though.

The next morning she took Amina up to see Miss Ellie, the schoolteacher.

'Miss! Miss! Amina and her little brother Bo want to come to our school. And the baby too, when she's a bit bigger. Would that be enough to keep it open?'

Miss Ellie said it just might be.

While the family stayed at her house and Amina and Bo started at school, Molly got the islanders to fix up one of the empty cottages for them.

Amina was thrilled, and so was her mother.

Meanwhile, more boats came past. Molly's father helped them, if they needed help. If they came to shore, the islanders gave them shelter.

And Amina waited. She watched and she waited.

Molly comforted her friend – she knew what it was like to be missing your dad.

A few days later, a man came from the mainland to take the new arrivals away.

'You can't take Amina or Bo!' cried Molly. 'They're my friends! And they need to stay here, for when their father turns up!'

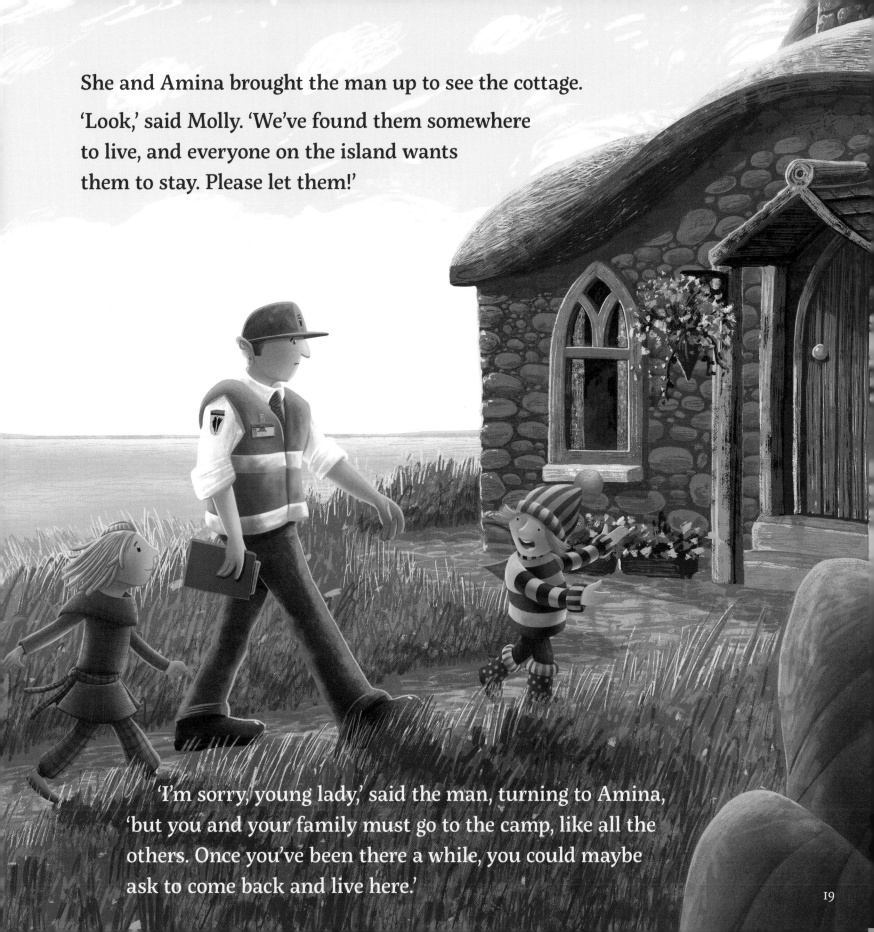

She and Amina brought the man up to see the cottage.

'Look,' said Molly. 'We've found them somewhere to live, and everyone on the island wants them to stay. Please let them!'

'I'm sorry, young lady,' said the man, turning to Amina, 'but you and your family must go to the camp, like all the others. Once you've been there a while, you could maybe ask to come back and live here.'

So Amina and her family left for the mainland, and the long summer passed. Molly and Amina sent postcards to one another.

'I hope you're OK, Amina,' wrote Molly. 'I watch for your father every day, but there's still no sign of him.'

'He is not here also,' Amina wrote back. 'They are
kind to us here, but the camp is very crowded.
I wish I was with you on the island.'

Molly kept a lookout as often as she could, but the weather had turned bad.

'Oh Amina,' she thought. 'I don't know how your father will ever find you now.'

Then one day, Molly spotted a boat on the rocks near the lighthouse. There was a man on it, waving frantically.

Red Hughie was down by the shore, fussing about with his rowing boat.

'Get her in the water, Hughie, quick!' yelled Molly. 'There's a boat breaking up out there!'

The waves were high, out on the open sea, but they managed to reach the sinking boat and help the man back to shore.

'My wife and children?' the man gasped as they staggered back up to Molly's house. 'Are they here?'

'Everyone's gone, I'm afraid,' Molly told him.

But there was something about this man – a look on his face.

'Amina? Bo?' Molly said to him.

The man's eyes lit up. 'Yes, yes!' he cried.
'You know them? Are they safe?'

'They were here,' she told him. 'But they've been
taken to the mainland. To the camp.'

'I must go!' said the man. 'I must go now!'

In the morning, Molly went down to the harbour with Amina's father, to wait for the first boat.

And there, to everyone's amazement and delight, was...

'Amina!' her father yelled.

'*Papi!*' cried his daughter, from the front of the boat, that was just arriving from the mainland.

'Yuri!' gasped Amina's mother, spotting her beloved husband. '*Mi bello* Yuri!'

'But...how...?' gasped Molly.

'Because we are back!' shouted Amina. 'They say we can live here now, with you!'

Now Amina's father helps Molly's dad with the fishing.

Amina's mum works in the school, helping Miss Ellie and the children.

If anyone on the island's ever hurt, it's great to have an extra nurse and an ambulance man around.

There are eight children in the school now. Well, eight and a half, really. And that's more than enough for it to stay open, says Miss Ellie. Which, as everyone agrees, is the best... news... EVER!

Malachy Doyle

Malachy Doyle grew up by the sea in Northern Ireland, and after living in Wales for many years has returned to Ireland. He and his wife Liz bought an old farmhouse on a small island off the coast of Donegal, where they live with their dogs, cats and ducks.

Malachy has had well over a hundred and twenty books published, from pop-up books for toddlers to gritty teenage novels. Over the years he has won many prestigious book awards, and his work is available in around thirty languages.

As well as the four previous stories in the Molly series, *Molly and the Stormy Sea*, *Molly and the Whale*, *Molly and the Lighthouse* and *Molly and the Lockdown*, his recent books include *The Miracle of Hanukkah*, *Rama and Sita*, *Jack and the Jungle*, *Big Bad Biteasaurus*, *A Hundred and One Daffodils*, *The Hound of Ulster* (Bloomsbury), *Fug and the Thumps* (Firefly Press), *Cinderfella* (Walker Books) and *Ootch Cootch* (Graffeg), which is illustrated by his daughter, Hannah Doyle.

Andrew Whitson

Andrew Whitson is an award-winning artist and Belfast native who likes to be called Mr Ando! He lives in an old house which is nestled discreetly on the side of a misty hill at the edge of a magic wood, below an enchanted castle in the shadow of a giant's nose. His house looks down over Belfast Harbour, where the *Titanic* was built, and up at the Belfast Cavehill, where an American B-17 Flying Fortress bomber plane once crashed during World War II!

Mr Ando makes pictures for books in the tower of a very old church and works so late that he often gets locked in. He has therefore forged a secret magic key which he keeps at his side at all times and uses to escape from the church when there is no one else around.

Mr Ando has illustrated over twenty books under his own name, the most recent of which being the Molly series with Malachy Doyle and the award-winning Rita series of picture books with Myra Zepf.